The Runaway Tortilla

Written by Eric A. Kimmel

Illustrated by Erik Brooks

WESTWINDS PRESS®

The Runaway Tortilla was originally published with artwork
by Randy Cecil by Winslow Press of Florida in 2000.

Second printing 2015

Library of Congress Cataloging-in-Publication Data

Kimmel, Eric A.
  The runaway tortilla / written by Eric A. Kimmel ; illustrated by Erik Brooks.
    pages cm
  Originally published in a slightly different form in Delray Beach, FL by Winslow
Press, 2000.
  Summary: In this Southwestern version of the Gingerbread Man, a tortilla runs
away from the woman who is about to cook him.
  ISBN 978-1-941821-69-5 (hardcover)
  ISBN 978-1-941821-88-6 (e-book)
[1. Fairy tales. 2. Folklore.] I. Brooks, Erik, 1972- illustrator. II. Gingerbread boy.
English. III. Title.
  PZ8.K527Ru 2015
  398.2—dc23
  [E]

                          2015006589

Art direction by Michelle McCann
Designed by Vicki Knapton

Published by WestWindsPress®
An imprint of

GRAPHIC ARTS
BOOKS®

P.O. Box 56118
Portland, Oregon 97238-6118
503-254-5591
www.graphicartsbooks.com

Once upon a time in Texas, down by the Rio Grande, there lived a couple known to all as Tía Lupe and Tío José.

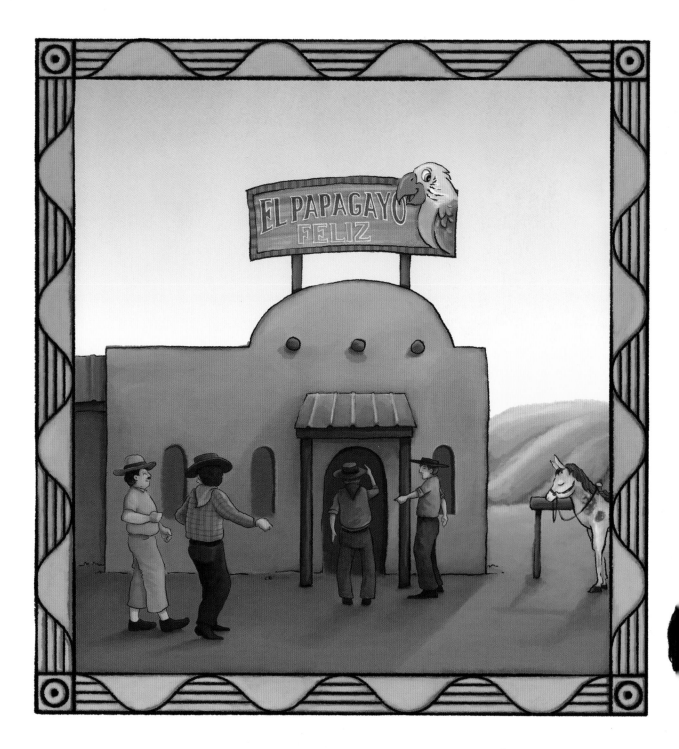

Tía Lupe and Tío José owned a taquería called El Papagayo Feliz, "The Happy Parrot." Cowboys came from near and far to eat there. Everyone said that Tía Lupe and Tío José made the best enchiladas, burritos, tacos, and fajitas in all of Texas.

The secret was the tortillas. Tía Lupe made each one by hand. They were as light as a cloud and as soft as the fuzz on a baby's cheek. "Tía Lupe," the cowboys warned, "you better not make these tortillas any lighter. Some day they'll up and run away!"

"Don't worry. That will never happen," laughed Tío José.

No sooner had he spoken when a tortilla jumped up and cried, "Oh yes it will! I'm too beautiful to eat!"

"I'm sorry, Tortillita," said Tía Lupe. "All tortillas are made to be eaten. That is what they are for."

"You'll have to catch me first," the tortilla exclaimed. She leaped from the griddle and ran out the door before anyone could catch her. Tía Lupe and Tío José chased after the tortilla, running as fast as they could.

"*Querida* Tortillita, come back! We promise not to eat you!"

"Promises, promises! I know what you want. But you won't get it," the tortilla yelled, running faster and faster.

And as she ran she sang:

"Run as fast as fast can be.
You won't get a bite of me.
Doesn't matter what you do.
I'll be far ahead of you!"

Through the streets and out of town ran the tortilla. She ran into the desert, where nothing grows but mesquite and cactus. Along the way she passed two horned toads basking on a rock.

"Come bask with us, Señorita Tortilla!" the horned toads cried.

"Lazy lizards! Catch me if you can!" the tortilla yelled.

"Run as fast as fast can be.

You won't get a bite of me.

Doesn't matter what you do.

I'll be far ahead of you!"

And away she ran, with two *sapos cornudos* scampering and Tía Lupe and Tío José running after her as fast as they could go.

Down the hill and past the cutbank ran the tortilla. She passed three donkeys braying.

"Hee-haw! Hee-haw! Come bray with us, Señorita Tortilla!"

"Silly burros! Catch me if you can!" the tortilla yelled.

"Run as fast as fast can be.
You won't get a bite of me.
Doesn't matter what you do.
I'll be far ahead of you!"

And away she ran, with three *burros* trotting, two *sapos cornudos* scampering, and Tía Lupe and Tío José running after her as fast as they could go.

Across the highway and over the bridge ran the tortilla. She passed four jackrabbits leaping over a mesquite bush.

"Come leap with us, Señorita Tortilla!" cried the jackrabbits.

"Foolish bunnies! Catch me if you can!" the tortilla yelled.

"Run as fast as fast can be.
You won't get a bite of me.
Doesn't matter what you do.
I'll be far ahead of you!"

And away she ran, with four *conejos* leaping, three *burros* trotting, two *sapos cornudos* scampering, and Tía Lupe and Tío José running after her as fast as they could go.

Around a wrecked car and through an old tire ran the tortilla. She passed five rattlesnakes shaking their rattles.

"Come make music with us, Señorita Tortilla," the rattlesnakes hissed.

"Rowdy rattlers! Catch me if you can!" the tortilla yelled.

"Run as fast as fast can be.
You won't get a bite of me.
Doesn't matter what you do.
I'll be far ahead of you!"

And away she ran, with five *cascabeles* slithering, four *conejos* leaping, three *burros* trotting, two *sapos cornudos* scampering, and Tía Lupe and Tío José running after her as fast as they could go.

Out and in and in and out of a box canyon ran the tortilla. She passed six cowboys loping along on their pinto ponies.

"Come ride with us, Señorita Tortilla!" the cowboys cried.

"Crazy cowboys! Catch me if you can!" the tortilla yelled.

"Run as fast as fast can be.
You won't get a bite of me.
Doesn't matter what you do.
I'll be far ahead of you!"

And away she ran, with six *vaqueros* galloping, five *cascabeles* slithering, four *conejos* leaping, three *burros* trotting, two *sapos cornudos* scampering, and Tía Lupe and Tío José running after her as fast as they could go.

Up and down, over and under, back and forth along winding desert trails ran the tortilla. One by one she left everyone behind.

Seis vaqueros.
Cinco cascabeles.
Cuatro conejos.
Tres burros.
Y dos sapos cornudos.

ven Tía Lupe and Tío José gave up and went home.

"I'll make another tortilla," Tía Lupe said.

"Cover the griddle so it doesn't get away this time," Tío José suggested.

But the tortilla didn't care. She ran along, faster and faster, even though no one was chasing her now. "Nobody can catch me!" she crowed. "I'm as fast as fast can be. No one is as fast as me!"

Suddenly she stopped. Up ahead, at the edge of an *arroyo*, she saw Señor Coyote. He sat on the sand with his mouth open. "Help me, Señorita Tortilla!" he moaned.

"What's the matter with you?" the tortilla asked.

Señor Coyote answered: "I was standing here by the edge of the *arroyo* with my mouth open when a grasshopper jumped in. He is caught in my throat. I cough and I cough, but I cannot get him out. Will you help me, Tortilla? Will you go down into my throat and pull out that wicked grasshopper?"

The tortilla answered, "Not I! How foolish do you think I am? I don't trust coyotes. I don't trust anyone."

Señor Coyote opened his mouth wider. "You don't have to be afraid of me, *cariño*. I can't hurt you. I'm not even hungry. Won't you help me? *Por favor.* Please!"

"What will you give me if I do?" the tortilla asked.

"Oh, Señorita Tortilla," Señor Coyote whispered, "I know where a great treasure is buried. I will take you there and share it with you if you pull this *chapulín*, this wicked grasshopper from my throat."

"Show me the treasure," the tortilla said.

"No way. First take out the grasshopper," Señor Coyote replied.

The tortilla ran into Señor Coyote's mouth. She looked around. "Where is this grasshopper? I don't see him."

"*¡Más hondo!* Go deeper!"

The tortilla ran past
Señor Coyote's tongue.
"I still don't see him."
"*¡Más hondo!* Go deeper!"

The tortilla ran past Señor Coyote's tonsils. She looked
down his throat. "There is no grasshopper here. I think you
are telling lies, Señor Coyote. You also have very bad breath!"
Señor Coyote confessed, "Have pity on me. I am so
hungry. I hoped that if I waited long enough with my mouth
open, something tasty might run in. And—I was right!"

Snap!

That was the end of the tortilla. And that is the end of the story. As for the treasure, it's still waiting for someone to find it. So all that's left is the song.

"Run as fast as fast can be.

You won't get a bite of me.

Doesn't matter what you do.

I'll be far ahead of you!"